DEREK JETER

BY BRIAN HOWELL

Printed in the United States of America,
North Mankato, Minnesota
112010
012011

 THIS BOOK CONTAINS AT LEAST 10% RECYCLED MATERIALS.

Editor: Matt Tustison
Copy Editor: Susan M. Freese
Interior Design and Production: Craig Hinton
Cover Design: Craig Hinton

Photo Credits: Henny Ray Abrams/AP Images, cover, title; Kathy Willens/AP Images, 4, 20; Frank Franklin II/AP Images, 7, 8; Chris O'Meara/AP Images, 10; The Canadian Press, Adrien Veczan/AP Images, 13; Richard Harbus/AP Images, 14; Mark Lennihan/AP Images, 17; Ron Frehm/AP Images, 18; Amy Sancetta/AP Images, 23; David J. Phillip, File/AP Images, 24; Evan Agostini/AP Images, 26; Kalamazoo Gazette, Jonathon Gruenke/AP Images, 29

Library of Congress Cataloging-in-Publication Data
Howell, Brian, 1974-
Derek Jeter : Yankee great / by Brian Howell.
p. cm. — (Playmakers)
ISBN 978-1-61714-747-0
1. Jeter, Derek, 1974—Juvenile literature. 2. Baseball players—United States—Biography—Juvenile literature. 3. New York Yankees (Baseball team)—Juvenile literature. I. Title. II. Series.

GV865.J48H69 2011
796.357092—dc22
[B]

2010040813

TABLE OF CONTENTS

Derek Jeter

ONE OF THE BEST

With the fans cheering, Derek Jeter swung the bat. He hit the ball down the line and into the outfield for a hit. Jeter had done that many times before. But this hit was special.

New York Yankees legend Lou Gehrig had 2,721 hits in his career. He played in the 1920s and 1930s. No player in team history had collected more hits until Jeter came along. Jeter's hit broke Gehrig's record, giving him 2,722 hits.

Derek Jeter became the Yankees' starting shortstop in 1996 and has been a star ever since.

"It's still hard to believe for me," Jeter said after breaking Lou Gehrig's record. "The way the fans have treated me around the city, at the field. . . . Being a Yankee fan, I never dreamt of this. The whole experience has been overwhelming."

Jeter had this hit against the Baltimore Orioles on September 11, 2009. The fans at Yankee Stadium stood and cheered for Jeter. His teammates ran onto the field to congratulate him. It was an unforgettable moment. But for Jeter, it was just one of many great moments in his career.

In 1996, Jeter became the Yankees' starting shortstop. Playing shortstop is an important job for a team. A lot of balls are hit to the shortstop's area of the field. The shortstop has to field the ball, make long throws, and make difficult plays in the field. The shortstop also often directs the other infielders. For most of his career, Jeter has been one of baseball's best shortstops.

Jeter tips his helmet to the home crowd on September 11, 2009. He had just broken Lou Gehrig's Yankees record for career hits.

Jeter dives into the crowd to make a catch against the Red Sox on July 1, 2004, at Yankee Stadium.

Through 2010, Jeter had helped the Yankees win the World Series five times. He was the American League (AL) Rookie of the Year in 1996. In 2010, he played in the All-Star Game for the eleventh time. Through 2009, Jeter had also received the Gold Glove Award four times for his outstanding defense.

Yankees fans have learned that Jeter will play hard every game. He proved that on July 1, 2004. That day, the Yankees

Through the 2010 season, Jeter had 2,926 hits in the regular season. He also had 185 hits in 147 career playoff games. No player in baseball history has had more hits in the playoffs than Jeter.

played the Boston Red Sox. The game was in the twelfth inning, tied at 3–3. Trot Nixon of the Red Sox hit a pop fly. Jeter sprinted to catch the ball. Running hard, he dove into the stands. He ended up getting cuts on his face, but he made the catch. Jeter's play helped the Yankees win the game.

Plays such as this have made Jeter a hero to Yankees fans. Babe Ruth, Joe DiMaggio, Mickey Mantle, and Gehrig are some of the greatest Yankees ever. Jeter belongs in that group too.

"The name Derek Jeter is made for stardom," said George Steinbrenner, the longtime owner of the Yankees, who passed away in 2010. "He's got an infectious smile, and he's so handsome and well-behaved. He's just a fine young man who does everything right."

NEW YORK

CHAPTER 2

HAVING A DREAM

Derek Jeter was born in New Jersey, just a few miles from Yankee Stadium. He was four years old when his family moved to Kalamazoo, Michigan. When he was a kid, he visited his grandparents in New Jersey during the summer.

Derek's grandmother, Dorothy Connors, was a Yankees fan. During one of Derek's visits, his grandmother took him to his first game at Yankee Stadium. He quickly became a Yankees fan.

Jeter makes a throw in 2010. As a child, Jeter dreamed of playing for the Yankees.

Derek's father, Charles, was a shortstop during his playing days. Derek decided to play shortstop because he wanted to be like his dad. Charles coached Derek for a few of his Little League years.

One day, when Derek was eight years old, he told his parents he was going to play for the Yankees. Throughout his childhood and his teenage years, he never gave up that goal.

Even when he played Little League baseball, Derek stood out. He had a strong arm. He also had great skills to make plays with his glove. Plus, Derek was a solid hitter and a fast runner. With these skills, he became a star player in Little League.

Derek loved other sports too. He enjoyed playing basketball and soccer. When he was in high school, he was one of the best basketball players in Michigan. But baseball was his favorite sport.

From a young age, Derek believed in setting goals. And his goals were always high. When he was a freshman in high school, he set the goal of becoming *USA Today*'s high school player of the year. Three years later, he was honored by *USA Today* as the nation's best player.

Jeter smashes a home run during the 2010 season. Jeter has been a good hitter ever since he played Little League baseball.

During Derek's junior year of high school, his batting average was .557. He also hit seven home runs. As a senior, his batting average was .508 and he hit four home runs.

The Yankees followed Derek throughout high school. "He always played one step ahead of where his age group was, and he still does," said Don Zomer, who was Derek's coach at Kalamazoo Central High School.

CHAPTER 3

BECOMING A YANKEE

Derek Jeter had a great senior season in 1992 at Kalamazoo Central High School. Shortly after the season ended, the Major League Baseball (MLB) Draft was held. The draft is an event in which major league teams select young players. High school and college players from around the United States are available to be drafted.

Most MLB teams knew about Jeter. Some people thought he would be taken first overall during

Minor leaguer Jeter, *left,* chats with the Yankees' Jim Leyritz, *middle,* and Mike Gallego in 1992.

the draft. The Yankees had the sixth choice. Jeter waited as five other players were drafted. With Jeter still available, the Yankees selected him. Jeter now had a chance to live his dream of playing for his favorite team.

Before he could make it to the major leagues, Jeter would have to work his way up through the minor leagues. He told his mom he wanted to become the minor league player of the year. But success didn't come easily. Away from home for the first time in his life, Jeter struggled during his first season as a professional. Looking back, he said,

> *I knew it was going to be an adjustment from high school to pro baseball. But I hadn't expected to feel as overwhelmed as I did. I hadn't imagined that I'd wind up crying in my hotel room night after night because I was playing so poorly.*

Jeter never lost sight of his goal, though. Friends and family told him to keep a positive attitude. During his second

Jeter poses in 1994. He is holding the trophy he won as *Baseball America*'s minor league player of the year.

Jeter smiles in 1996 after he was named the AL Rookie of the Year for his play with the Yankees.

year in the minor leagues, Jeter played much better. And in his third year as a pro, he was named minor league player of the year by several publications.

Then, on May 28, 1995, Jeter got the call he had been waiting for. The Yankees were bringing him to the big leagues. Jeter flew on a plane to Seattle, Washington, to meet the team. His father, Charles, also flew to Seattle to watch his son play.

During his rookie season in 1996, Jeter hit .314 for the Yankees. He had 10 home runs, 78 runs batted in, and 14 stolen bases. He got every first-place vote in the voting for AL Rookie of the Year.

The next day, Jeter played his first game for the Yankees. He was 20 years old. It didn't matter that he failed to get a hit that day. He had made it! In his second game, Jeter got his first hit.

"I think we should all set goals in life and set them high," Jeter has said. "I did that, and my parents encouraged me to do it, which is one of the main reasons I am where I am today."

In 1995, Jeter played in only 15 games for the Yankees. But in 1996, he became the team's starting shortstop. That was a great season for Jeter. He was named the AL Rookie of the Year. He also helped the Yankees win the World Series over the Atlanta Braves.

CHAPTER 4

BECOMING CAPTAIN

When the Yankees won the World Series in 1996, they had many excellent players. Tino Martinez, Paul O'Neill, and Bernie Williams were some of the best players in the AL. The Yankees had great pitchers too.

Derek Jeter was just 22 years old. But he was the best rookie in the league. He was also one of the best players on the team. Yankees manager Joe Torre knew he could depend on Jeter. Jeter's teammates counted

Jeter celebrates during the 1996 playoffs. As a rookie, he helped the Yankees win the World Series.

on him too. "When he first came here, the other players seemed to gravitate toward him," Torre said. Jeter had become a star because he always played hard.

Jeter was the Most Valuable Player (MVP) of MLB's All-Star Game in 2000. He was also the MVP of the World Series. He became the first player in baseball history to win both awards in the same season.

During Jeter's career, the Yankees have been one of the best teams in baseball. They have had many star players, but Jeter has been the team's leader. He helped them win the World Series in 1998, 1999, and 2000. After five years in the majors, Jeter had already won four World Series rings. The kid from Kalamazoo seemed to have it all.

But since 2000, winning hasn't come as easily for Jeter and the Yankees. Through 2010, they had been to the playoffs in 14 of Jeter's 15 full big-league seasons. But they didn't always meet their goal of winning the world championship. From 2001 to 2008, the Yankees failed to win the Series.

Jeter holds up four fingers in 2000 after he won his fourth World Series with the Yankees.

Jeter's strong play continued, however. He finished second in voting for the MVP Award in 2006. He also made the All-Star team six times from 2001 to 2008.

In 2003, Jeter's leadership was rewarded by his own team. The Yankees named him team captain. The Yankees have not always had a captain. Jeter was the first one in eight years. He has been the captain ever since.

Mariano Rivera, *right,* and Jeter smile after the Yankees won the 2009 World Series. It was the team's fifth title with Jeter.

Jeter's hard work has continued throughout his career. In 2009, he and the Yankees saw their hard work pay off when they reached the top again. Jeter finished third in the MVP voting. He also helped the Yankees win the World Series for the fifth time in his career. New York beat the Philadelphia Phillies. When the 2009 season was over, Jeter was given another honor.

As of 2010, Jeter was still the Yankees captain. Only one other player has held this position as long as Jeter. Roger Peckinpaugh was the Yankees' captain from 1914 to 1921. Baseball Hall of Famers Babe Ruth and Lou Gehrig have also been Yankees captains.

He was named Sportsman of the Year by *Sports Illustrated* magazine.

As a child, Jeter dreamed of playing baseball for the Yankees. Now he is one of the greatest players the sport has ever seen. He still loves the game as much as he did as a kid. He has said,

> *I only wanted to play baseball. I only wanted to play shortstop. I only wanted to play for the Yankees. My whole life. This has always been the dream of mine: to play shortstop for the New York Yankees. And I get a chance to do it.*

www.michaeljfox.org
www.michaeljfox.org

CHAPTER 5

GIVING BACK

Derek Jeter has become a hero to many fans for his work on the baseball field. He has also become a hero for what he has done off the field.

When Jeter was a rookie in 1996, he created the Turn 2 Foundation. The foundation helps kids in western Michigan, New York City, and Tampa, Florida. Turn 2 helps kids have a healthy lifestyle. It rewards them for their good work in school. It also

Actor Michael J. Fox, *left,* and Jeter pose in 2008 at a charity benefit for Parkinson's disease.

rewards them for their leadership and positive behavior. Since Turn 2 began, it has raised more than $11 million and helped thousands of kids.

Bud Selig is the commissioner of MLB. He has had high praise for Jeter and his work on and off the field. "You're a wonderful role model not only for the youth of America, but also for our players," Selig told Jeter.

Jeter has written a book that includes life lessons for kids. He tells kids to set high goals and not to be afraid to fail. He also tells them to find positive role models and to put strong people around them. Jeter encourages kids to have fun but also to be serious about life. He teaches many other lessons as well.

In 2009, Jeter was honored with the Roberto Clemente Award. It's an award that recognizes an MLB player who excels on the field and gives back to the community. Jeter's work with the Turn 2 Foundation was a big reason he won the award.

Starting Turn 2 back in 1996 was important to Jeter. Today, his family helps a lot with the foundation because he's

Jeter and 11-year-old Dontre McGee smile in 2007 at a Turn 2 Foundation gathering in Kalamazoo, Michigan.

busy playing baseball. Jeter's younger sister, Sharlee, is the foundation's president. It's no surprise that she has become so involved. Derek and Sharlee's parents taught them to give back to others. "If you have more than you need, share it with someone else," Sharlee has said. "[Derek] is just doing what he was raised to do."

FUN FACTS AND QUOTES

- As a kid, Derek Jeter's favorite baseball player was Dave Winfield. Winfield played for the Yankees through much of Jeter's childhood, from 1981 to 1990. Winfield was voted into the Baseball Hall of Fame in 2001. He was also very involved with charity work. That influenced Jeter to start the Turn 2 Foundation.
- Growing up, Jeter was a very good basketball player. As a teenager, he got a chance to play against two future stars: Chris Webber and Jalen Rose. Both players went on to play at the University of Michigan and then in the National Basketball Association (NBA).
- "You gotta have fun," Jeter has said of baseball. "Regardless of how you look at it, we're playing a game. It's a business, it's our job, but I don't think you can do well unless you're having fun."

WEB LINKS

To learn more about Derek Jeter, visit ABDO Publishing Company online at **www.abdopublishing.com**. Web sites about Jeter are featured on our Book Links page. These links are routinely monitored and updated to provide the most current information available.

GLOSSARY

adjustment
A change or modification.

batting average
A baseball statistic that tells how good a player is at hitting the ball. If a player gets four hits in ten times at bat, he has a batting average of .400.

captain
The leader of a group.

draft
In baseball, an event held every year in which teams rotate in selecting new players.

encourage
To give someone hope or confidence.

goal
Something a person wants to achieve.

infectious
Able to spread or to be shared.

league
In sports, a group of teams or clubs. Professional baseball teams are part of Major League Baseball (MLB). The MLB is divided into the American League (AL) and the National League (NL).

overwhelmed
Feeling troubled or helpless, often because of being under a lot of stress or pressure.

professional
In sports, someone who is hired and gets paid to play his or her sport.

stardom
Being famous, such as an athlete or celebrity.

INDEX

FURTHER RESOURCES

Hopkinson, Deborah, with Terry Widener. *Girl Wonder: A Baseball Story in Nine Innings*. New York: Aladdin, 2006.

Jeter, Derek, with Jack Curry. *The Life You Imagine: Life Lessons for Achieving Your Dreams*. New York: Three Rivers Press, 2001.

Mills, Clifford W. *Baseball Superstars: Derek Jeter*. New York: Chelsea House, 2007.

Roth, B. A. *Derek Jeter: A Yankee Hero*. New York: Grosset & Dunlap, 2009.